Unicorn Princesses
SUNBEAM'S SHINE

The Unicorn Princesses series

Sunbeam's Shine

Flash's Dash

♕

Coming soon

Bloom's Ball

Prism's Paint

Breeze's Blast

Moon's Dance

Unicorn Princesses
SUNBEAM'S SHINE

Emily Bliss

illustrated by **Sydney Hanson**

BLOOMSBURY
NEW YORK LONDON OXFORD NEW DELHI SYDNEY

First published in the United States of America in August 2017
by Bloomsbury Children's Books
www.bloomsbury.com

Bloomsbury is a registered trademark of Bloomsbury Publishing Plc

For information about permission to reproduce selections from this book, write to
Permissions, Bloomsbury Children's Books, 1385 Broadway, New York, NY 10018
Bloomsbury books may be purchased for business or promotional use.
For information on bulk purchases please contact Macmillan Corporate and
Premium Sales Department at specialmarkets@macmillan.com

Library of Congress Cataloging-in-Publication Data
Names: Bliss, Emily, author. | Hanson, Sydney, illustrator.
Title: Sunbeam's shine / by Emily Bliss ; illustrated by Sydney Hanson.
Description: New York : Bloomsbury, 2017. | Series: Unicorn princesses ; 1
Summary: A human girl visits the Rainbow Realm, an enchanted land ruled by
a circle of unicorn princesses, to help Princess Sunbeam regain her
magical powers.
Identifiers: LCCN 2016036842 (print) | LCCN 2016050236 (e-book)
ISBN 978-1-68119-326-7 (paperback) • ISBN 978-1-68119-325-0 (hardcover)
ISBN 978-1-68119-327-4 (e-book)
Subjects: | CYAC: Unicorns—Fiction. | Princesses—Fiction. | Magic—Fiction.|
BISAC: JUVENILE FICTION/Animals/Mythical. | JUVENILE FICTION/
Fantasy & Magic. | JUVENILE FICTION/Royalty.
Classification: LCC PZ7.1.B633 Su 2017 (print) | LCC PZ7.1.B633 (e-book) |
DDC [Fic]—dc23
LC record available at https://lccn.loc.gov/2016036842

Book design by Jessie Gang
Typeset by Westchester Publishing Services
Printed and bound in the U.S.A. by Berryville Graphics Inc., Berryville, Virginia
2 4 6 8 10 9 7 5 3 1 (paperback)
2 4 6 8 10 9 7 5 3 1 (hardcover)

For Phoenix and Lynx

Unicorn Princesses

Princesses

SUNBEAM'S SHINE

Chapter One

In the top tower of Spiral Palace, a green wizard-lizard waved his wand at an orange ear of corn. He took a deep breath. And then he chanted, "Alakazam! Alakazoop! Unicorn, unicorn! Alakaboop!" He waited for the ear of corn to turn bright pink. But instead, the lights flickered and the walls shook. Thunder rumbled and boomed. Blue and green lightning flashed across the sky, which had grown dark as night.

"Oh dear! Oh dear!" the wizard-lizard cried out. "Did I say 'unicorn, unicorn'? I meant 'ear of corn, ear of corn'! Oh dear!" The wizard-lizard turned pale green. He frantically waved his wand at the ear of corn and yelled, "Undo! Undo! Cancel that spell! Delete! Erase! I take that one back!"

But the palace lights kept flickering. The thunder rumbled even louder. Yellow and silver lightning flashed.

"Oh, not again!" the wizard-lizard exclaimed. "The unicorn princesses are going to be so angry this time. They told me to stop casting spells on vegetables." He raced over to the window just as a glittering yellow sapphire rose up into the sky. Then, with one final burst of thunder, the brightly colored stone dropped into a shimmering, purple canyon in the distance.

"That was Princess Sunbeam's magic gemstone," the wizard-lizard said, covering his face with his scaly hands. "Without it, Sunbeam doesn't have any magic powers. Now I've really done it!"

The wizard-lizard leaped over to a box in the corner of the room. He pulled out a book, looked at the cover, and tossed it aside. He pulled out another book and threw it. And then another. Finally, he found the right book. In silver letters, the title read, *The Book of Unspells*. The wizard-lizard leafed through the pages, muttering, "Oh dear, oh dear! Princess Sunbeam has lost her magic, and it's all my fault!"

He read out loud from a page at the back of the book, "There is only one way to reverse a spell that robs a unicorn princess of her magic gemstone. A human girl who believes in unicorns must travel to the Rainbow Realm, find the lost gemstone, and return it to the princess. Only then

will the princess regain her magic powers.
Note: Only human girls who believe in unicorns are able to see them." The wizard-
lizard's eyes filled with excitement.

"We need a human girl! And one who
can see unicorns!" he cried out as he raced
from the room and down the palace's spiral staircase to find the unicorn princesses.

Chapter Two

One Saturday afternoon, Cressida Jenkins was on a hike in the woods with her family. Her parents walked up ahead, and her older brother Corey followed just behind them. He looked through a pair of binoculars. "I see a hawk!" he called out. "Oh, wait. It's just another crow."

What Cressida really wanted to see,

much more than a crow, or even a hawk, was a unicorn. Her parents had told her many times unicorns weren't real. "They're imaginary, honey," her mother would say. Cressida always nodded, but she couldn't help but wonder if her mother might be wrong.

Real or imaginary, if there was one thing Cressida loved, it was unicorns. Posters of pink and purple unicorns covered her bedroom walls. She had a unicorn bedspread, unicorn curtains, and a unicorn lamp on her bedside table. Her pink book bag had a picture of a unicorn on the back. She even had unicorn pencil erasers for school and silver unicorn sneakers with pink lights that blinked when she walked, jumped, and ran. In art class, she had painted six unicorn watercolor pictures. They all hung on the refrigerator next to the week's school-lunch menu and Cressida and Corey's soccer game schedules.

Cressida's father turned around right in front of the biggest oak tree Cressida had ever seen. "It's time to head back," he said. "We need to get home in time to go to the grocery store before dinner." Cressida sighed. She didn't want to go home yet, even if the only birds were crows and there were no unicorns. Plus, she hated going to the grocery store. No matter what Cressida said or did, her parents wouldn't buy Frosted Marshmallow Unicorn-Os cereal. The box was pink and shiny with a picture of a gigantic purple unicorn leaping from a cereal bowl. "It's too sugary," her father always said as he pushed the cart right past the Unicorn-Os. Then he usually pulled a boring, brown box of Whole Wheat Squares off the shelf.

As Cressida turned to follow her parents and Corey back to their house, she looked down at her sneakers and jumped. The blinking pink lights always cheered her up.

Just then, Cressida glimpsed something shimmering in a pile of leaves near the gigantic oak tree. She stepped to the side of the path, reached down, and picked it up. It was a long, old-fashioned key. But the strangest part about it was the handle, a sparkling, pink crystal ball.

"Honey," Cressida's mother called out. "Did you find something?"

"Just an old key," Cressida said. And she slipped it into her pocket.

♔

That evening as she got ready for bed, Cressida pulled her favorite green unicorn pajamas from her dresser drawer. As she started to take off her jeans, she felt something heavy and pointy. She stuck her hand into her pocket and wrapped her fingers around the key. She had forgotten all about it!

As Cressida cupped the key in her hands, she noticed the crystal ball on the handle now glowed emerald green. Had she imagined the ball was pink that afternoon?

"Huh," she said. She put the key on her dresser, next to a unicorn statue she had made from pipe cleaners and milk cartons.

When Cressida's mother came to tuck her in, she saw the key. "What a strange key!" her mother said. "It's beautiful!"

"When I found it, the handle was pink," Cressida said.

"That's odd," her mother said. Cressida could tell from her mother's voice she didn't believe her. It was the same tone she used when she told Cressida that unicorns were imaginary. "It was probably just the sunset reflecting on the glass."

"Hmm," Cressida said, but the more she thought about, the surer she felt the handle had been pink.

Chapter Three

A s soon as Cressida woke the next morning, she jumped out of bed and grabbed the key off her dresser. Now the crystal ball was blue, the color of the ocean! Was her mother right that the light made the ball look different colors? Cressida opened her curtains and switched on her unicorn lamp. But even in the crisp, clear morning sunlight, the ball glowed dark blue.

She stared at the key for a long time. Did it fit into the gate of a secret, magic garden? Or unlock a treasure chest? Or open a castle door? Maybe it belonged to a

fairy or a witch or even a troll. And then she whispered out loud, "What if whoever dropped this key in the woods goes back to look for it? What if they need it and are trying to find it?"

Cressida suddenly felt guilty she had taken it. Maybe she should have left it there, in the pile of leaves. She decided she should return it as soon as possible.

She quickly put on her favorite outfit: black jeans, a green dress with a unicorn on the front, bright yellow socks, and her blinking unicorn sneakers. She left a note for her parents saying she went for a walk and would be home in time for breakfast. And then she raced out the door, through her backyard, and into the woods where her family had walked the day before. Cressida sprinted along the forest path, her sneakers blinking, until she got to the giant oak tree.

Cressida kneeled down and reached into her pocket for the key. She decided to leave it sitting on a root of the oak tree instead of under the pile of leaves where she found it. That way, it would be easier to see.

Just then, Cressida heard a rustling noise behind her. And then a high voice, unlike any she had ever heard, said, "Oh, I know I left it here. I know I did. Where is it? I'll never get home!"

Cressida sucked in her breath. The voice didn't sound like it belonged to a human.

She turned around slowly. And then she
froze. Cressida couldn't believe her eyes.
Right in front of her, five feet away, was
what looked like a yellow pony. Its coat
was the color of a buttercup, and it had
gold hooves, a silky blond mane, and—a
shiny gold horn! It wasn't a pony, Cressida realized as she drew in her breath. It
was a unicorn!

Cressida pinched herself. The unicorn
was still there.

She closed her eyes, counted to five, and
opened them again. The unicorn was still
there.

She pinched herself so hard she whispered, "Ouch!" The unicorn was *still* there.

Cressida watched, her mouth open and

her eyes wide, as the unicorn rummaged through the leaves with her nose and hooves. A necklace made of blue ribbon hung around the unicorn's neck. Cressida noticed a large hole in the ribbon, and she wondered if something that had been attached to the necklace was missing.

"Oh, where is it?" the unicorn said again.

"Are you looking for this?" Cressida asked, holding the key out in front of her. Now the ball glowed pink again.

The unicorn reared up and stepped backward. With large, dark eyes she looked down at the key. An enormous grin spread across her face. "The key!" she whinnied. "Thank you!" Then, with

her mouth, she took the key from Cressida's hand. Cressida's heart skipped a beat. A unicorn's nose had just brushed against her skin.

♛

Then the unicorn froze. She looked at Cressida, narrowed her eyes, and dropped the key between her hooves. "Wait a minute!" the unicorn said. "Can you see me?"

"Of course," Cressida said. It seemed like an awfully strange question.

"Are you absolutely sure?" The unicorn flicked her blond mane and twitched her blond tail.

"Of course I'm sure!" Cressida said, laughing. "You're standing right in front of me. You just touched my hand with your nose."

"You can see me! You can see me!" the unicorn sang out, dancing in a circle and rearing up on her hind legs. "You're a human girl who believes in unicorns!"

"Well," Cressida said, giggling, "yes, I suppose that's true."

"You must come back with me to the Rainbow Realm," the unicorn cried. "Please say you will! And by the way, my name is Princess Sunbeam."

"Back to where?" Cressida asked. "And you're a princess? Should I curtsy?"

"Don't bother curtsying," Sunbeam laughed. "The Rainbow Realm is a magic land ruled by my sisters and me. Usually, we stay away from the human world, but I have a little bit of a problem. Well, actually a big problem. And I really need your help."

"What's wrong?" Cressida asked. She tried to imagine what kind of problem a royal unicorn could have.

"I bet you noticed that hole in my necklace," Sunbeam said, crossing her eyes and looking down toward her chest.

Sunbeam's face looked funny, but Cressida managed to nod instead of laugh.

"My magic yellow sapphire, which gives me my special power, is gone. Without it, I might as well be a pony with a golden horn!" Sunbeam exclaimed dramatically.

Now Cressida couldn't help but giggle. When she caught her breath, she asked, "How did you lose your yellow sapphire?"

Sunbeam sighed. "Well, there's this wizard-lizard—his name is Ernest—who lives in our palace. And when he gets bored, he amuses himself by casting spells on the fruits and vegetables. Usually he tries to turn them different colors, just for fun, but sometimes he tries to change them into spiders and butterflies. We've asked him to stop because his spells always go wrong. Always. But he never listens. And so this time, he accidentally cast a spell that made my yellow sapphire fly off. Now it's lost, and the only way to reverse the spell is for a human girl who believes in unicorns to find my magic gemstone and return it to my necklace. Ever since yesterday morning, I've been in your world, walking right up to human girls. And they've stared through me, like I'm made of air. That's because they don't believe in unicorns. You're the first one who has been able to see me. I'd given up, and I was ready to go home. And then I found you while I was looking for my key."

Cressida smiled with delight. "My mother keeps telling me unicorns are imaginary. But I've always known unicorns are real."

"My mother used to tell me humans smell funny," Sunbeam said, pushing her nose toward Cressida and inhaling loudly. Cressida suddenly wished she had taken a bath that morning. After several seconds of sniffing, Sunbeam said, "My mother was wrong! You don't smell bad at all."

Cressida giggled with relief.

"So," Sunbeam said, "will you come back to the Rainbow Realm and help me find my magic gemstone?"

Cressida's heart swelled with excitement. And then she remembered her parents, who would worry if she wasn't home soon. "The only thing," she said, "is I left my parents a note saying I'd be back in time for breakfast."

"No problem," said Sunbeam. "Human time will freeze while you're in the Rainbow Realm. When you come back out, it will be exactly the same time as when you came in. You'll be back in plenty of time for breakfast."

"Well," Cressida said as her heart

thundered in her chest. She couldn't remember ever feeling so excited and nervous. "What are we waiting for?"

Sunbeam reared up and whinnied with excitement. "Fantastic!" she said, and then she lowered down onto her knees. "Climb onto my back."

"I've never ridden a unicorn, or even a pony," Cressida said.

"Well, I've never been ridden before," Sunbeam said. "Hold on to my mane, and we'll figure it out together."

Carefully, Cressida climbed onto Sunbeam. The unicorn's back was warm, soft, and surprisingly steady. Her mane felt like threads of silk in Cressida's hands. Sunbeam stood, picked up the key with her mouth,

and trotted over to the oak tree. Then she pushed the key into a tiny hole Cressida had never noticed in the tree trunk. Suddenly, the forest began to spin. It whirled faster and faster, until the trees were just a green and brown blur. Cressida gripped Sunbeam's mane as tightly as she could.

And then she had the feeling the two of them were falling. It was like being in an elevator hurtling downward without stopping at any floors.

With a jolt, the spinning and falling stopped. Cressida blinked. They were in one of the biggest, grandest rooms Cressida had ever seen. Purple velvet curtains hung from floor-to-ceiling windows. Crystal chandeliers sent rainbow light all over the white marble floors. Along one wall were silver troughs filled with water and something else that looked, Cressida thought, like honey or maple syrup. Harp music played softly, and silver candles burned in glass holders.

"Welcome to Spiral Palace," Sunbeam said.

Chapter Four

Sunbeam kneeled, and Cressida slid sideways off Sunbeam's back. Her sneakers' pink blinking lights reflected on the shiny white floor. She closed her eyes and breathed in. The air smelled like pine trees and lavender.

"Get ready to meet the other unicorn princesses," Sunbeam whispered. She winked at Cressida before she called out,

"Hey, everyone! I'm back! And guess what I found?"

Cressida heard the sharp clatter of hooves against the marble tiles. And then six more unicorns, each a different color and each wearing a gemstone necklace, were standing in the room.

"These are my older sisters," Sunbeam said to Cressida. "The silver one is Princess Flash. Her magic power is to run so fast lightning bolts shoot from her horn and hooves. The green one is Princess Bloom. Her magic power is to make things grow and shrink. The purple one is Princess Prism. She paints beautifully and can change the color of any object. The blue

one is Princess Breeze. She can make the strongest gusts of wind you can imagine. The black one is Princess Moon. Her power is to make everything dark as night. And the orange one is Princess Firefly. She can create swarms of fireflies and make things glow."

The unicorn princesses swished their tails and flicked their manes as they stared at Cressida with wide, unblinking eyes.

"It's wonderful to meet you," said Cressida. "I'm Cressida Jenkins. I'm not a princess. I don't have any magic powers. But I sure am excited to be here." Cressida curtsied just for fun. She couldn't imagine another time she might have the occasion to curtsy in front of a herd of unicorn princesses.

Flash stepped forward with a serious expression on her face. A diamond, attached to a pink ribbon around her neck, shimmered in the light of the chandelier. "Are you absolutely and positively sure you see us?" she asked.

"Yes," Cressida said.

Flash sniffed several times. Then she turned to Sunbeam and whispered, just loud enough that Cressida could hear, "Isn't it odd that she doesn't smell? I was expecting to have to open some windows and turn on a fan."

Sunbeam whispered back, "I know. I

thought I'd have to hold my nose the whole time I was in the human world. But it turns out humans don't really smell. At least, most of them don't."

"Interesting," Flash whispered, and then the two sisters looked at Cressida. Cressida pretended she hadn't heard them as she tried not to giggle. She decided not to mention that human boys, especially her brother, often smelled terrible.

"Cressida," Flash said, "has Sunbeam explained to you her situation with the wizard-lizard and the magic spell?"

"Yes," Cressida said. She wanted to ask if she would get to meet the wizard-lizard, too. She was curious to find out what, exactly, a wizard-lizard looked like. But when she saw Flash's icy eyes, she decided to ask Sunbeam about the wizard-lizard later.

"Did Sunbeam tell you about the different domains inside the Rainbow Realm?"

"The domains?" Cressida said. "I don't think so."

Flash frowned.

"I was getting to that," Sunbeam said. And then she whispered to Cressida, "Flash is the oldest sister. Nothing I do is ever good enough for her." Cressida nodded in sympathy. She knew exactly what it felt like to be a younger sister.

"Well, allow me to explain," Flash said in a tone Cressida associated with her teachers at school.

Sunbeam rolled her eyes and snorted.

Flash sighed and continued, "Our mother, Queen Mercury, divided up the Rainbow Realm so that each princess could have our own land, or domain, to rule over. She decided which princess would get which domain based on our magic powers. Since Sunbeam's power is to create heat and sun, she rules over the Glitter Canyon. Our best guess is that Sunbeam's yellow sapphire is in the canyon. I know it's a lot to take in all at once. Does that make sense to you?"

Cressida nodded to show she understood.

"Are you sure?" Flash asked. "I can explain it all again."

"I've got it," Cressida said. She wondered if Flash thought human girls weren't very smart. Perhaps Queen Mercury had told her daughters that humans were both smelly and dumb.

"Very well," Flash said. "Are you willing to go to the Glitter Canyon this morning to look for Sunbeam's yellow sapphire?"

"Absolutely," Cressida said. She felt a surge of excitement. She had never been to a canyon before, and certainly not one that glittered.

"Splendid," Flash said, and she smiled. "Have you had breakfast?"

Cressida suddenly realized she was very hungry. She hadn't eaten since dinner the night before. "Not yet," she said.

Flash used her mouth to pick up and ring a silver bell. Almost as soon as it made a soft tinkling noise, five scarlet dragons, each wearing an apron and a chef's hat, whistled as they walked in pushing gold troughs on wheels. Threads of blue smoke and tiny green flames danced from their nostrils.

"Thank you," Flash said.

"No problem," one of the dragons said as green fire erupted from his mouth.

"Dragons are great cooks," Sunbeam whispered into Cressida's ear. "They don't even need stoves or ovens because they breathe fire. And they can cut our fruit using their claws instead of knives."

Cressida nodded as she watched the

dragons leave the room, their red tails dragging along the floor. "I had no idea dragons were real, too," she said.

"Of course they are," said Sunbeam, shrugging. "Anyway, I'm starving. Let's have some breakfast."

Inside the troughs were what looked like slices of purple-and-pink striped tomatoes with teal seeds alongside piles of what looked like cookies made with hay and orange berries instead of oatmeal and raisins. The unicorns dipped their mouths into the troughs and began to noisily chew. Cressida watched, unsure of what to do. Was she supposed to get on her hands and knees and eat from the trough, just like the unicorns? To her relief, one of the dragons

returned with a silver
platter piled high
with striped
fruits.

"Thank you
so much," Cressida
said, taking the tray.

Cressida's stomach
growled as she bit into the fruit. It was the
freshest, juiciest fruit she had ever had. She
decided it tasted like a cross between a
kiwi, a fresh peach, and a coconut. The
little blue seeds were crunchy and sweet,
like toffee.

"What is the name of this fruit?" Cressida asked Sunbeam. "It's amazing!"

"Those are giant roinkleberries from

Bloom's garden. She's an amazing gardener! She uses her magic power to make the fruit grow and the weeds shrink."

Bloom nodded as she chewed a roinkleberry. The emerald on her necklace glittered. "It's a good thing I can use magic to grow my fruits and vegetables. Now that Sunbeam's yellow sapphire is gone, there's no sun for my garden."

"Now that I've found Cressida, that should change soon enough," Sunbeam said. "I'm sure she'll find my yellow sapphire in no time."

"I'll do my very best," Cressida said. She felt a little nervous. What if she couldn't find the gemstone? "I can do this," Cressida whispered to herself. And then she took a deep breath and ate another bite of her roinkleberry. After she felt full— roinkleberries were quite filling—she slipped a roinkleberry in her jeans pocket, just in case she felt hungry later.

As soon as the unicorns finished eating, Sunbeam jumped up, full of energy. "Well, let's go!" she said. "I can't wait to show you Glitter Canyon." Then Sunbeam whispered to Cressida, "And I'm ready for a break from Flash. I love her, but my oldest sister drives me crazy sometimes!"

Cressida smiled. "I know the feeling. I have an older brother."

Sunbeam kneeled down, and Cressida climbed onto her back.

"Good-bye!" Sunbeam called to her

sisters, trotting in an excited circle. "The next time you see me, I'll have my yellow sapphire and my magic powers back."

Sunbeam swished her tail and, with Cressida still perched on her back, trotted toward the palace door. "Good luck!" the unicorn princesses called out after them.

"Sunbeam," Flash called out, "no fooling around. You and Cressida have serious work to do!"

Chapter Five

Outside the glass door, Sunbeam trotted along a path of clear, shining stones that led away from the castle and toward a thick pine forest. For a moment, Cressida turned and looked behind her at Spiral Palace. She knew, right then, how it had gotten its name: the princesses' home was shaped

like a giant, white, glittering unicorn horn, and spiraled up toward the sky. "Wow," Cressida whispered.

As soon as they were out of sight of the palace, Sunbeam ran faster and reared up, laughing as she jumped and played. "Whoa!" Cressida yelled, wrapping her arms around Sunbeam's neck. But she couldn't help giggling as Sunbeam danced in circles.

"Don't let Flash get to you," Sunbeam said. "She's way too serious. There's plenty of time to have fun today, even while we're searching for my yellow sapphire." The princess sped up and leaped over a pine tree that had fallen across the path. "I'm just excited to be out of that hot, stuffy palace with that silly harp music and those smelly candles." Sunbeam whinnied as she jumped over several more fallen trees. Then she began to gallop, and for several minutes Sunbeam raced along a narrow, winding forest path. Finally, she slowed down. "We're almost to the Glitter Canyon!" she announced.

Sure enough, the forest was getting thinner, with fewer and fewer trees. "Close your eyes!" Sunbeam called out. "I can't wait for you to see the canyon! You're going to love it!"

Cressida shut her eyes. She felt Sunbeam speed up, and she tightened her grip on the unicorn's mane. Suddenly, the air felt much cooler, as though Sunbeam had just walked into a refrigerator. Cressida shivered.

"Okay! Now you can look!" Sunbeam called out, her voice high with excitement. Cressida opened her eyes and sucked in her breath. She and Sunbeam stood on the edge of a beautiful purple canyon. At the top were towers of gigantic plum-colored rocks, patches of lavender grass, fields of violets, and pebbles that looked like silvery grapes. Down at the bottom of the canyon were clusters of cacti in every shade of purple Cressida could imagine, and sand that looked just like the purple glitter she used in art class at school. Cressida had never seen so much purple in her life!

"Welcome to the Glitter Canyon!"

Sunbeam sang. "It's my very own part of the Rainbow Realm!" Sunbeam kneeled down, and Cressida slid off her back.

"This is incredible," Cressida said. "It's the most beautiful place I've ever seen."

"It's even more beautiful when the sun is in the sky," Sunbeam said, sighing. "And it's much, much warmer. You'll be amazed by how gorgeous it looks once you find my yellow sapphire and I can make the sun come out."

That's when Cressida noticed there was something strange about the light in the canyon. The purple sand didn't shine, even though it looked like glitter. The cacti didn't have any shadows. And the light seemed dim, as though it were a cloudy day, even though the sky was completely clear. Cressida looked up at the sky. The sun was missing! No wonder it was so cold. Cressida shivered and rubbed her arms. She wished she had brought her winter coat.

Just then, Sunbeam ran forward, danced in a circle, and said, "Come on! Let's go down to the bottom of the canyon. We can start looking for the yellow sapphire there."

Cressida and Sunbeam walked together along a path that led to the bottom of the canyon. Lizards, turtles, and frogs the color of grape jelly climbed and hopped on the towers of rocks, and light purple parakeets perched in the branches of silvery purple trees.

As they hiked, Cressida felt a sudden

burst of heat. And then something small and red scampered across the path and disappeared behind a rock. At first, Cressida thought it was a chipmunk. But when it crossed the path again, this time closer to Cressida and Sunbeam, Cressida could see it looked just like a red and orange candle flame with flailing arms, legs, and a tail.

"Yikes!" Cressida called out. "What is that?"

"Oh, that's a flame-bite," Sunbeam said. "Just make sure it doesn't touch you. And make sure you don't drop any roinkle-berry seeds on the ground. Flame-bites love roinkleberry seeds so much they'll follow you around for days hoping you'll feed them."

The flame-bite darted behind a bush with plum-colored leaves. And then it scampered out, right in front of Cressida and Sunbeam. It shrieked and scurried in circles, so its arms, legs, and tail danced in every direction. Cressida jumped backward. She shielded her eyes from the flame-bite's bright light. Beads of sweat formed on her forehead from the flame-bite's heat.

"Shoo!" Sunbeam said. "Go away!" The flame-bite screeched and ran away. "They're not dangerous, but they sure are annoying," Sunbeam said. "At least they go away as soon as you tell them to." As soon as the flame-bite left, the cold returned. Cressida shivered and hoped the bottom of the canyon would be warmer.

Chapter Six

B y the time Sunbeam and Cressida hiked to the bottom of the canyon, Cressida was so cold her teeth were chattering.

"It's pretty chilly," Cressida said, touching her arms, which were covered in goose bumps. "You don't have a coat I could wear, do you?"

"Hmm," Sunbeam said. "Unicorns

don't really wear coats, so I don't have one
for you to borrow. Some of my sisters like
to wear capes, but the Glitter Canyon is
usually so hot that I don't have one. Not
that it would fit you anyway."

Just then, out of the corner of her eye,
Cressida saw something the color of egg
yolks amid all the purple. She turned and
there, hanging on a lavender cactus, was a
furry yellow jacket and yellow boots with
a fuzzy lining. Both were exactly the color
of Sunbeam.

"Look at that!" Cressida said. She and
Sunbeam walked over. On the jacket hung
a sign that said, Dear Cressida, Thank you
for your help. Sincerely, Ernest.

"Ernest?" Cressida said, hurriedly

putting on the coat. "That's the wizard-lizard, right?"

"Yes," Sunbeam said. "I bet he meant to make the coat and boots purple, and they came out yellow." They both giggled.

Cressida took off her blinking unicorn sneakers and put on the yellow boots. "How do I look?" she asked. She twirled around in a circle.

"Fabulously yellow!" Sunbeam exclaimed. "But still not quite as yellow as I am."

Cressida felt much warmer now that she had her coat and boots.

"Well," she said, eyeing the rocks and sand and cacti. "I guess we better start searching for your sapphire. Where have you already looked?"

Sunbeam blushed and glanced down at her hooves. "The truth is I haven't started. I just don't even know where to begin. It could be anywhere."

Cressida nodded. She looked at the stretch of purple sand in front of them.

And the mounds of purple rocks. And the clusters of purple cacti. There must have been millions of cracks, crannies, and crevices where a yellow sapphire could be hiding. She could see exactly what Sunbeam meant. It was hard to decide where to begin. Cressida took a deep breath. She knew from doing school assignments that the only way to finish a big project was to do a little bit at a time.

"Let's start by searching down here, at the bottom of the canyon. Why don't you go over there and use your hooves to look through the sand?" Cressida pointed to a stretch of sand next to several scraggly purple pine trees. "And I'll go over here and sift through the sand with my hands."

Cressida pointed to a stretch of sand on the other end of the canyon, next to several cacti.

"Sounds good!" Sunbeam said. She trotted over to the pine trees and began to dig with her hooves and nose.

Cressida walked over to the cacti and sat down in the purple sand. It felt cold through her jeans, and she was grateful that the wizard-lizard had thought to make a warm coat and boots magically appear. Cressida grabbed a handful of sand and let it slide through her fingers. Then she grabbed another handful. And another.

Just then, she thought she heard a noise that sounded like chuckling. She stopped and looked around. She didn't see anyone.

Maybe it was the desert wind, Cressida thought. She shrugged and grabbed another handful of sand. She heard the laugh again. But this time the same voice said, "Oh golly! Oh gee! That tickles!"

Cressida looked all around her. That time she was sure it wasn't the wind. Then she noticed the ground shaking slightly. Cressida grabbed one more handful of sand. The laugh was even louder, and the ground trembled even more. "Oh golly golly gee!" the voice cried out. "That tickles!"

"Who's there?" Cressida asked. She wondered if some magic canyon creature was hiding behind a cactus.

"It's Danny," the voice said. "Danny the Dune."

"Danny the Dune?" Cressida asked. "Where are you?"

Danny the Dune laughed. "You're sitting on me," he said. Cressida looked down. All she saw was purple sand. And then the sand beneath her trembled, and the laughter grew even louder. Suddenly, the ground underneath her rose up, so she was sitting atop a small hill. Right below her legs, two big violet eyes opened and a purple mouth curled into a smile.

"Tricked ya, didn't I?" Danny said. "I bet you didn't know you were sitting on a dune!"

Cressida giggled with delight. "What's a dune?"

"It's a sand hill. You've probably seen us

at the beach. Or maybe the last time you visited the desert." Cressida didn't have the heart to tell Danny the Dune she had never been to the desert. And she'd only been to the beach once, when she was five. She didn't remember it well enough to know if she'd seen any sand dunes. "A few of us dunes live here, at the bottom of the Glitter Canyon."

"I'm sorry I keep tickling you," Cressida said. "I'm looking for Sunbeam's yellow sapphire. Have you or any of the other dunes seen it?"

Danny made a strange growling noise. "Well," he said. "I heard from Denise, who heard from Darryl, who heard from Doris, who heard from the twins, Dave and Devin, that the cacti have the yellow sapphire. They're hiding it from everyone. On purpose." Cressida figured that Denise, Darryl, Doris, Dave, and Devin were all dunes.

"The cacti?" Cressida said. "Do the cacti talk, too?"

"Well," Danny said, sounding even angrier, "the cacti *can* talk. And they used to talk to us all day long. But after we told them to give the yellow sapphire back to Sunbeam, they told us they didn't have it. And then they stopped talking to us. It's awfully lonely down here in the canyon without any cacti to talk to."

"Hmm," Cressida said. She could hear not just anger, but also hurt in Danny's voice. He sounded like he missed his friends. And she also got the feeling there was more to the story than what Danny had told her. "Would you mind if I tried to talk to the cacti?" she asked.

"Be my guest," Danny said. "Maybe they'll tell you where they're hiding the yellow sapphire."

Chapter Seven

Cressida stood up and brushed sand off her coat, her jeans, and her boots. Just like glitter, the sand stuck to everything.

Cressida tiptoed over Danny, trying not to tickle him with her feet, though he chuckled each time she pressed her boot into the ground. She climbed over a pile of rocks that looked like giant eggplants, and stopped in front of a shivering purple cactus with its arms folded tightly across its chest.

"Hello there," Cressida said, and she smiled her kindest, friendliest smile.

The cactus blinked and frowned. Its teeth were chattering and its lips had a bluish tinge.

"I know you're really cold," Cressida said, "but would you be willing to talk to me just for a moment?"

"It depends," the cactus snarled. "Did the dunes send you up here?"

"No," Cressida said. "I've come on my own. My name is Cressida Jenkins. Princess Sunbeam brought me here to find the yellow sapphire."

The cactus stared at Cressida for a long

time and sighed. "I'm Corrine," she finally said. She unfolded one of her arms, smiled, and reached a prickly hand out toward Cressida. After a few seconds, Cressida realized the cactus wanted to shake her hand. Careful to avoid Corrine's needles, Cressida used her thumb and index finger to take the cactus's hand. "With a name like Cressida, you could be a cactus," Corrine said. "All our names begin with *C*."

"I'd love to be a cactus like you," Cressida said, trying to be polite. But truthfully, Cressida thought being a cactus sounded terrible. She would hate to be rooted to one place in the ground, even if it meant living with unicorn princesses in the Rainbow Realm.

"I'm relieved you've come to find Sunbeam's yellow sapphire," Corrine said. "We're all freezing cold. And we can't just put on a coat the way you can."

"That sounds awful," Cressida said. "I'll find the sapphire as soon as I possibly can. And that's why I came to talk to you. Do you have any ideas about where I should look?"

"The dunes are hiding the sapphire on purpose," Corrine sniffed. "Though you'll have to be the one to ask them where it is. The cacti aren't speaking to them."

"Why aren't you speaking to them?" Cressida asked. She wanted to hear the other side of the story.

"Well," Corrine said, crossing her prickly

arms even more tightly, "they kept accusing us of hiding the yellow sapphire on purpose. When we told them for the hundredth time that we don't have it, the dunes called us liars. And then they said our needles are dull and our flowers are ugly. That's when we quit talking to them." Cressida thought the fight between the dunes and the cacti sounded like the arguments she had with her brother Corey.

"I see," said Cressida. She wanted to be careful not to take sides. "Wait, did you say you have flowers?" Cressida asked, looking more carefully at the cacti. She didn't see a single flower.

With one of her arms, Corrine pointed to several green lumps on her head and chest. "These are our flowers. We can only open them in the sun," Corrine explained. "As soon as the wizard-lizard cast his spell, all our flowers shut."

Cressida looked at the three other shivering cacti standing near Corrine. Sure enough, they were all covered in the same green lumps.

"What color are your flowers?" Cressida asked. She imagined the cacti looked brilliant in the sunlight, with their flowers open.

"Mine are magenta," Corrine said proudly.

"Mine are blue," another cactus said. "I'm Claude, and it's a pleasure to meet you."

"Mine are pink," said another. "I'm Carl."

"Mine are yellow," said one more, who, Cressida noticed, looked worried. "I'm Callie."

"It's a pleasure to meet all of you. And I bet your flowers are beautiful," Cressida said. "I promise I'll find Sunbeam's gemstone as soon as I can."

"Thank you," the cacti said in unison.

"Have any of you actually seen the yellow sapphire?" Cressida asked.

"Of course not," Corrine, Claude, and Carl replied in unison. Cressida noticed Callie said nothing. Instead she cast her eyes downward and frowned nervously. Cressida thought Callie looked like she had a secret, and Cressida wondered if that secret was about the yellow sapphire.

Cressida walked over to Callie and leaned in as close to Callie's ear as she could without getting prickled. "Callie?" she whispered. "Can I ask you a question?"

Callie tightened her shivering arms. She looked so worried Cressida thought she might start crying. Cressida wanted to give her a hug, but that didn't seem like a good idea, given the long, sharp purple needles that covered Callie's body.

"I'm wondering if you know anything about where the yellow sapphire could be," Cressida whispered.

"What are you two whispering about?" Corrine called out. Callie's eyes widened.

"Nothing!" Cressida called back. And then to Callie she whispered, "Any secrets you have are safe with me."

"Do you promise not to tell Corrine, Claude, and Carl?" Callie whispered.

"I promise not to tell anyone anything without your permission," Cressida answered.

Callie took a deep breath and blinked back several tears. "Well, on the day Ernest cast the spell, it was very strange here in the Glitter Canyon. There was thunder and lightning. The sky got dark. And then the sun vanished. Just then, I felt something hard and heavy land in one of my flowers. At first I thought it was one of the purple rocks that are all over the canyon. But just before my petals shut, I caught a glimpse of something yellow and glittery. I'm almost positive the sapphire is inside one of my closed flowers, but I can't open it without the sun." Callie took a deep breath. "I'm afraid to tell the other cacti because they're so sure the dunes have the yellow sapphire. And I'm afraid to tell the dunes because they're already so angry at us. I've been afraid to tell Sunbeam because she's the princess, and I don't want her to get mad at me."

Cressida felt thrilled she had almost surely found the yellow sapphire, but concerned for Callie. "Thank you so much for trusting me," Cressida whispered. "Don't worry. We'll find a way to get the sapphire out of your flower. But I do think I'd better tell Sunbeam."

"Do you think she'll be angry?" Callie asked.

"I don't know for sure," Cressida said, "but I doubt it. And even if she is, I bet you two will be able to work it out."

"Well," Callie said. She bit her lip and furrowed her brow. "Okay. You can tell Princess Sunbeam."

"Thank you," Cressida said. And with that, she ran across the canyon as fast as she could, all the way back to Sunbeam.

"Sunbeam!" she cried out, breathless. "Guess what?"

Sunbeam dropped a long purple stick from her mouth and raised her head. Cressida glanced down at the sand by the unicorn's hooves and saw that Sunbeam had been drawing pictures of suns, rainbows, and girls riding unicorns. "My eyes were so tired from looking at the purple sand that I was worried that even if the yellow sapphire was right in front of me, I wouldn't see it. I decided to take a break," Sunbeam explained. "Did you find it?"

"I know where it is," Cressida said, and she told Sunbeam about her conversation with Callie.

"Good job," Sunbeam said. "I knew a girl who believes in unicorns could find it." The unicorn furrowed her brow. "Now we just have to figure out how we can get the yellow sapphire out of Callie's flower. Without the sun, she can't open it."

"Hmm." Cressida had hoped Sunbeam would have an idea.

Just then, a flame-bite scampered in front

of Sunbeam and Cressida. For a moment it stood still, and Cressida squinted and shielded her eyes from the flame-bite's bright light. After only a few seconds, she felt as though she had stepped into a hot oven, and she unzipped her yellow coat. Suddenly, the flame-bite squealed and scurried in circles around Sunbeam, flailing its arms and legs as it ruined her drawings.

"Shoo!" Sunbeam said, stamping her hoof. The flame-bite shrieked one last time and dashed behind a violet-colored pine tree. Immediately, the cold returned.

"Rats!" Sunbeam said. "That silly flame-bite ruined the best picture I've ever drawn of a human girl. Before I met you, I always thought humans had tails."

Cressida laughed. And then, as she zipped back up her coat, she had an idea. "Sunbeam," she said slowly, "how high can flame-bites jump?"

"They can't jump at all," Sunbeam said. "They just run around and shriek."

"And you said they like roinkleberry seeds?" Cressida asked.

"They love roinkleberry seeds. They'll do almost anything to get them."

Cressida pulled the roinkleberry from her pocket, split it in half, picked a teal seed from the center, and threw it as far away from them as she could.

"Good throw," Sunbeam said, admiring how far the seed had sailed.

For a few seconds, the seed lay in the

sand. Then a flame-bite scurried from a pile of rocks and popped the seed into its mouth. As soon as it finished chewing, it screeched and ran in circles, searching for more.

"Watch out," Sunbeam said. "If it thinks you'll feed it, it will follow us everywhere." Fortunately, the flame-bite didn't realize Cressida had thrown the seed, and it darted back behind the rocks.

"I've got a plan!" Cressida exclaimed, jumping up and down. "But we'll have to get the cacti and the dunes to work together."

Sunbeam swished her tail and frowned. "I doubt that will work," she said. "They've had arguments before, but I've never seen them this angry."

"I know they're angry," Cressida said, thoughtfully, "but I think it's possible they can be friends again. Every time my friends and I have gotten into an argument, we've found a way to talk about it and make up. If they didn't still care about each other, they wouldn't feel so angry and hurt."

Sunbeam raised one yellow eyebrow and shrugged. "I guess we can try!" she said. "What should we do first?"

"Hmm," Cressida said. "The first step is to go talk to Callie."

"Climb on!" Sunbeam kneeled, and Cressida quickly climbed onto the unicorn's back.

Chapter Eight

Sunbeam galloped across the Glitter
Canyon, her gold hooves kicking up
a cloud of purple dust behind them.
As the cold wind rifled through Cressida's
hair, she closed her eyes and smiled. There
was nothing in the world better than riding
a unicorn, she decided.

Sunbeam stopped on the other side of

the canyon, right in front of Corrine, Claude, Carl, and Callie.

Callie glanced at Cressida with a look of panic. Cressida smiled reassuringly at the nervous cactus, slid off Sunbeam's back, walked over to Callie, and leaned as close to Callie's ear as she could. "I have an idea for how to get your flower to open," Cressida whispered, "but we'll need the dunes to help us. Could I have your permission to tell the other cacti and the dunes what happened?"

Callie took a deep breath and said, with a wavering voice, "If we need to tell everyone, I'd like to do it myself."

"That's very brave," Cressida replied.

Callie took another deep breath. She looked at Corrine, Claude, and Carl. And then she looked down at the six purple sand dunes—Danny, Denise, Darryl, Doris, Dave, and Devin. "I have something important to say," she announced.

The other cacti, who were whispering among themselves, stopped their conversations and looked up. But the dunes frowned, closed their eyes, and began to slide away. Then Danny yelled, "We're not talking to the cacti until they admit they're holding the yellow sapphire on purpose!"

"We don't have it! You do!" Claude snarled back. "You're just jealous that we have flowers and you don't. You're

Sunbeam said. The dunes closed their sandy purple mouths. The cacti shut their bluish-purple, prickly lips. Sunbeam looked at Callie. "Go ahead," she said.

"Well," Callie said, "I think the yellow sapphire is stuck in one of my flowers."

Doris muttered, "I knew it!"

Callie continued, "I promise I haven't been holding it there on purpose. It landed there when the wizard-lizard cast his spell. A̲ ̲ ̲ ̲ ̲my flower closed, and I couldn't open it. I ̲ ̲ ̲ ̲id to say anything because I didn't want to ̲ ̲ ̲e the fight between the dunes and the cacti wo̲ ̲ ̲ ̲sorry for not telling you sooner. I didn't kno̲ ̲ ̲o do."

The dunes grumbled among ̲ ̲ ̲n-selves, but Cressida could tell they felt les̲ angry. They could hear in Callie's voice that she was telling the truth: she wasn't hiding the yellow sapphire on purpose, and she wanted to get it out of her flower—and back on Sunbeam's necklace—as quickly as possible.

Finally, Danny said, "We're sorry we said all those mean things to you. We just felt frustrated."

"And cold," said Darryl. "I'm always mean and cranky when I'm cold."

Corrine laughed. "Me too," she said.

"Yes, me too," Claude and Carl added.

There was a long silence, and Cressida held her breath.

Danny cleared his throat. "Friends again?" he asked.

✳ ✳ ✳

"Yes, friends again," Corrine said.

When all the dunes and all the cacti smiled and cheered, Cressida exhaled. She felt a warm, full feeling in her heart.

"I feel much better now," Callie said. Then she looked at Cressida. "But I'm still really cold. Didn't you say you have a plan to get my flower to open?"

"I sure do," Cressida said. "For my plan to work, we all have to work together. Are you ready?"

They all nodded.

"Great," Cressida said. "First, I need all the dunes to get in a circle around Callie and to lie as flat as possible." The dunes looked puzzled, but they slid over to Callie and arranged themselves in a tight circle.

They flattened and closed their eyes and mouths.

"Perfect!" Cressida said. "When I yell, 'Up!' I need you to get as tall as possible, so tall that you're like a wall around Callie. And I need you to stay like that until I yell, 'Got it!' Can you do that?"

"Yes," Danny, Denise, Darryl, Doris, Dave, and Devin all said in unison.

"Fantastic," Cressida said. Then she looked at Sunbeam. "Would you mind standing right here?" Cressida pointed to the sand behind Danny. "If it's okay with you, I'll need to sit on your back."

"Sure," Sunbeam said, looking confused as she walked over to Danny.

Cressida winked at Sunbeam and

smiled reassuringly at Callie. And then she pulled the roinkleberry from her pocket and picked out a handful of seeds. She placed a seed on Danny's forehead, and another one a few inches away on his nose. She kept putting down roinkleberry seeds until she had made a trail leading across Danny and right up to Callie. Then, in front of Callie's closed flower, she left a pile of seeds.

Cressida ran over to Sunbeam, climbed onto her back, and whispered, "Now we just have to wait."

Soon enough, a flame-bite, running and shrieking, found the first seed Cressida had placed on the ground. It crouched down, popped the seed into its mouth, and then moved on to the next seed, and then the next, moving closer and closer to Callie. When it found the pile of seeds right in front of Callie, it began cramming them into its mouth.

"Up!" Cressida called out.

The dunes rose up as high as they could, surrounding Callie and the flame-bite with a high, sandy wall. In the flame-bite's heat and light, Cressida noticed Callie's flower had started to open just a little bit. Her plan was working!

When the flame-bite gobbled up the last of the seeds, it began to shriek and run in circles, trying to get away. But the dunes were too steep, and it was trapped right in front of Callie. Cressida watched as Callie's flower kept slowly opening.

The dunes panted and grunted. "How much longer?" Dave and Devin groaned.

Cressida looked at Callie's flower. It was halfway open. "You're doing an amazing job!" she yelled. "Just a little longer! You can do it!"

The flame-bite screeched even more frantically. Cressida pushed her hand into her pocket, and, to her relief, she found several more seeds that had fallen out of the roinkleberry. She tossed them right in front of Callie, and the flame-bite stuffed them greedily into its mouth. Callie's flower opened a little more. And then a little more. Now Cressida could see the yellow sapphire. "If I climb up on your neck, could you please get me as close to Callie's flower as possible?" Cressida asked Sunbeam.

"Of course," Sunbeam said, and she craned her neck toward Callie.

Meanwhile, Danny cried, "I don't think I can stay like this much longer!"

"You can do it! We're almost there!" Cressida exclaimed. She slid onto Sunbeam's neck and leaned forward. Then she reached her left arm toward the yellow sapphire. But when she tried to grab it, her fingertips barely brushed the gemstone. She wasn't quite close enough.

"Hold on tight!" Sunbeam whispered.

Then, with a whinny, Sunbeam reared up onto her hind legs and thrust her front legs and head toward Callie's flower.

"Whoa!" Cressida yelled as she reached

again for the yellow sapphire. This time, she closed her hand around the cold, hard gemstone, and yelled out, "Got it!"

"Phew!" all six dunes yelled as they flattened to the ground, breathing hard and groaning. The flame-bite, shrieking and flailing, raced away.

"That was the hardest work I've ever done!" Darryl panted.

"You're telling me!" Denise said, trying to catch her breath.

Cressida scooted down Sunbeam's neck and onto her back before she slid to the ground. The yellow sapphire felt smooth and heavy in Cressida's hand, and she opened her fingers to see it up close. It shimmered in her palm.

"Good job, everyone!" Cressida said. "That was really hard, and you did it." Then she looked over at Sunbeam. "Are you ready to get your sapphire back?"

Sunbeam smiled with excitement and nodded. She bent her neck toward Cressida, and Cressida carefully placed the yellow sapphire in the empty circle in Sunbeam's blue necklace. Suddenly, Sunbeam's horn began to shimmer, and a brilliant ray of light came out from the tip. Sunbeam whinnied with joy.

The sun, bright and yellow, appeared in the sky. Soon, it was so warm that Cressida peeled off her yellow jacket and rolled up her sleeves. She fanned herself as she beheld the beauty of the Glitter Canyon. The sand glittered. The cacti, their prickles shining and their flowers opening, unfolded their arms and raised them toward the sky. The shimmering dunes slid and danced. A brilliant blue sky replaced the dim, gray one.

"Thank you, Cressida," Sunbeam said. "You've done an amazing job. You worked hard, and that hard work has paid off."

"I was happy to help," Cressida said. And she meant it.

"Let's go back to the palace!" Sunbeam said. "I can't wait to tell my sisters what you did!" She kneeled down, and Cressida climbed onto her back.

Chapter Nine

Back at the palace, the unicorn princesses crowded around Cressida. "Wow!" Flash said after Sunbeam told her sisters how Cressida had recovered the yellow sapphire from Callie's flower. "I had no idea human girls were so creative and smart."

Cressida smiled proudly.

"Amazing," said Bloom.

"Incredible," Prism added, nodding, so the amethyst on her necklace glittered.

Breeze, Moon, and Firefly flicked their manes and tails in agreement, and Cressida admired how beautiful all their gemstones looked in the brightly lit palace.

Then Flash looked at Sunbeam and whispered, so loud Cressida could hear her, "Do you want to give it to her, or do you want me to?"

"I'll do it," Sunbeam whispered. Flash nodded, though she looked disappointed.

Sunbeam turned and trotted down a long hallway with marble floors and chandeliers. Soon, she reappeared with a pink velvet pouch in her mouth.

"We, the princess unicorns, have a special

gift just for you," Flash said. The other unicorns fell silent and smiled.

Sunbeam walked right up to Cressida and dropped the pink pouch into her hands. Cressida's heart fluttered with excitement. She immediately recognized the shape of the gift inside the pouch. Grinning, she pulled out the key with the glowing crystal handle.

"It's your very own key to the Rainbow Realm!" Sunbeam exclaimed.

"We'd very much like you to have it," said Flash. Bloom, Prism, and all the other unicorns nodded.

"You're welcome to visit anytime you want," Sunbeam said. "And when we want to signal for you to return, we'll make the handle turn bright pink. Do you remember where the key goes, in the big oak tree?"

"Yes, I remember," said Cressida, wondering how she could ever forget that. "Thank you!" It was the best present she could imagine. She already couldn't wait for her next visit to the Rainbow Realm.

Just then, her stomach rumbled, and she realized she was hungry for more than just roinkleberries. And even though she didn't think she would tell her parents or Corey about her adventure—she knew they wouldn't believe her—she missed them. As if Sunbeam could read her mind, the unicorn said, "I bet you're ready to go home."

Cressida nodded. "I've had such an

amazing time here," she said. "But I should get back to my family. They'll be expecting me for breakfast."

"Anytime you're ready to leave the Rainbow Realm, all you need to do is close your eyes, put both hands on the handle of the key and say 'Take me home!'" Flash explained. "Why don't you try it now? And we'll see you again soon."

Cressida nodded. She waved good-bye to Flash, Bloom, Prism, Breeze, Moon, and Firefly. As she hugged Sunbeam, she said, "I'm so glad I could help you." She put both hands on the key's handle and closed her eyes. "Take me home!" she said. And then she added, "Please!"

Right away, Cressida felt a spinning

sensation. She opened her eyes. For an instant, she saw a blur of purple, silver, and white before everything went pitch black. This time, instead of a falling sensation, Cressida felt as though she were soaring upward. And then the flying sensation stopped, and the spinning slowed until she could see she was in the woods outside her house, lying on the ground next to the giant oak tree. For a moment, Cressida stared at the morning sky, with the puffy white clouds and the crows cawing from the tree branches. Finally, she sat up. She looked down at her key—her very own key to the Rainbow Realm—with its blue crystal handle, and slid it into her pocket. As she stood up, she noticed her yellow boots were gone, and she was yet again wearing her silver unicorn sneakers with the pink lights.

Cressida took a deep breath. She smiled. And then she ran home for breakfast with her parents and Corey, her unicorn sneakers blinking all the way.

DON'T MISS OUR NEXT MAGICAL ADVENTURE!

TURN THE PAGE FOR A SNEAK PEEK . . .

In the top tower of Spiral Palace, Ernest, a green wizard-lizard, placed two avocados in a bowl. He smoothed his cape and straightened his pointy purple hat. With one scaly hand, he opened a thick, dusty book entitled *Intermediate Spells for Enterprising Wizard-Lizards.* With the other hand, he clutched a silver wand.

He cleared his throat. And then, reading from the book as he waved his wand at the avocados, he chanted, "Stickety Snickety Battery Goo! Pinkity Spinkity Strawberry Spew! Sleetily Sweetily Thickily Slew!" He waited. Nothing happened to the avocados. They didn't even quiver or jump.

"Huh," Ernest said. He repeated the spell. Again, nothing happened.

He wrinkled his brow and scratched his head. Then he checked his book. "Oh dear! Oh dear!" he muttered. "I read the wrong spell. Again. Oh dear! I thought that one sounded awfully strange."

Ernest rushed over to the window. Usually, when he cast the wrong spell, the sky darkened, thunder boomed, and lightning flashed. But this time the sun still shone in the cloudless blue sky above the Rainbow Realm. Just as he was about to breathe a sigh of relief, Ernest saw two bright pink clouds hovering over the Thunder Peaks. The clouds glittered and sparkled above the gold and silver mountains. And then, in a burst of light, the clouds vanished.

"Oh dear! I've done it again," Ernest muttered. "I guess I'll have to tell Flash." He sighed, scratched his head, and looked back at the avocados. He leafed through his book to find the spell he had meant to read, "Instructions for Turning Avocados into Flying Sneakers." And then, waving his wand, he chanted, "Fleetily Speedily Fastily Foo! Wing Feet, Fleet Feet, Fast Feet, Blue!"

The two avocados trembled and spun in circles. They turned from purple to red to blue. And then, with a flash of gold so bright Ernest had to shield his eyes, two blue running shoes, each with a set of gold wings, appeared on the floor. Ernest jumped with excitement and slid his scaly feet into the shoes.

"I did it! I did it!" he called out as he sprinted back and forth across the room. "Thunder Dash, here I come!"

Emily Bliss lives just down the street from a forest. From her living room window, she can see a big oak tree with a magic keyhole. Like Cressida Jenkins, she knows that unicorns are real.

Sydney Hanson was raised in Minnesota alongside numerous pets and brothers. She has worked for several animation shops, including Nickelodeon and Disney Interactive. In her spare time she enjoys traveling and spending time outside with her adopted brother, a Labrador retriever named Cash. She lives in Los Angeles.

www.sydwiki.tumblr.com